Dinosaur

Coloring Book for Kids

This book belongs to

....

Lawrence Niington

Thank you

We hope you enjoyed our
dinosaur coloring book.
As a small family company, your
feedback is very important to us.

Please let us know how
you like our book at:

lawrenceniington@gmail.com